For Margaux
SA-L

For my sister
Claire-Grandcœurdemiel
AV

MYRIAD BOOKS LIMITED
35 Bishopsthorpe Road, London SE26 4PA

First published in 2004 by

MIJADE PUBLICATIONS
16-18, rue de l'Ouvrage 5000 Namur-Belgium

© Sylvie Auzary-Luton, 2004
© Anne Velghe, 2004

Translation Lisa Pritchard

ISBN 1 905606 23 0

Printed in China

Neighbour BEAR

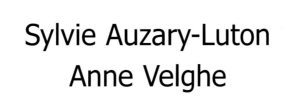

Sylvie Auzary-Luton

Anne Velghe

MYRIAD BOOKS LIMITED

One winter's day when the snow lay thick on the ground, Little Bear lay in his bed dreaming of honey. Lots and lots of lovely honey…

He woke up feeling very hungry.
So he got up and went into the kitchen.
And what do you think he ate?

HONEY.

Then he went back to sleep in his warm bed.

And every time Little Bear woke up,
he ate some more honey.

But one evening Little Bear ate his last pot of honey. He searched his cupboard just in case there was one more pot. But…

There was no more honey at all.

"Oh dear," he said. "I hope it's nearly spring."

He knocked on Mouse's door.
"MOUSE! MOUSE! I've eaten up all my honey.
Is it spring yet?"

Mouse peeked out: "No, Little Bear, it's still winter."

Little Bear sighed: "But I've eaten all my honey and I am very hungry.
When will it be spring?"

"Oh, you'll have to wait
another two months," said Mouse.
"Would you like a pancake?"

"Yes please," said Little Bear.

So Mouse fetched a tiny pancake on a tiny plate.

"Eat it up and go back to sleep," she told Little Bear. "Time flies when you are asleep."

"Thank you, Mouse. That was delicious," said Little Bear. And he went back to bed.

Little Bear closed his eyes. He tossed and turned. But however hard he tried, he couldn't go back to sleep.

"I'm a bear," he sighed. "I'm supposed to sleep all winter. Spring won't come for another two months."

He counted all the bees on his curtain. Then he counted them again. But it was no good, he was still wide awake.

"Maybe Mouse will make me some cocoa to help me sleep."

Little Bear stood at Mouse's door and called: "MOUSE! MOUSE!
Are you there?"

Mouse was very sleepy. "Shhh! Do be quiet! You'll wake everyone in the
forest!"

Little Bear sighed: "I can't sleep. Would you please make me a cup of cocoa?"

Mouse brought him a tiny cup of cocoa.
Little Bear swallowed it in one gulp, and asked for more.

"Could you put some honey in it too?" he said.

But Mouse had had enough. She was very tired and wanted to go back to bed.

"No more now. GO TO BED!" she said, and closed her door.

But Little Bear still couldn't sleep. So he went out to find his friends in the forest.

"Oh my! So this is snow! I never knew it was so beautiful!"

And he jumped
and he sang

and he laughed
and he rolled in the snow.

Little Bear heard a scrunching in the snow. There was Hedgehog, looking very grumpy.

Little Bear said: "I'm very hungry but I've run out of honey. Do you have something I could eat?"

"Well," muttered Hedgehog. "I have a few dried slugs."

And before he had finished speaking, Little Bear had gobbled them all up.

Hedgehog was very cross. "YOU ARE SO GREEDY! Now I have no food left."

Little Bear said he was sorry. " I will go and find you some more right now."

"SILLY LITTLE BEAR!" exclaimed Hedgehog. "You won't find slugs in winter. We'll have to wait till spring."

Little Bear clambered up Squirrel's tree. "Squirrel, are you awake?" he called.

"I was having a lovely sleep," Squirrel said crossly. "Why aren't you asleep, Little Bear?"

"Hedgehog wants some slugs… and a pot of honey too," said Little Bear.

"All I've got is these hazelnuts," said Squirrel.

Quick as a flash, Little Bear gobbled them all up.

"You are so GREEDY! Now I have no food left!" cried Squirrel.

But Little Bear wasn't listening. He sang at the top of his voice as he skipped in the snow.

Badger was not impressed. "DO BE QUIET! You're waking everybody up. Why don't you go back to bed?"

"I'm so hungry, Badger! Do you have anything to eat?" asked Little Bear.

"Just this little pot of blackberry jam," said Badger.

Quick as a flash, Little Bear gobbled it all up.

Badger was very cross. So were Squirrel and Hedgehog.

Beaver came out to see what all the commotion was about.
"What's up?" he said.

"Little Bear has eaten all our food!" they all cried.
"He is so greedy."

Then Fox came strolling by.

"I'm glad to see you! I was just on my way to warn you that there is a big bear out in the forest, carrying a big bag."

Badger was worried. "Maybe it's a burglar."

Squirrel said crossly, "Little Bear's eaten everything up. There's nothing left to steal."

Hedgehog was scared. "Maybe the big bear is coming to eat us all up."

Whatever should they do?

Squirrel climbed up the tree to take a look.
"It's over there! The big bear is going in to Little
Bear's house."

"Be careful, Little Bear. It may be dangerous."

All the animals slowly tiptoed towards Little Bear's
house. Squirrel held Little Bear's paw and they both
went up to the front door.

The door was open! Squirrel peeped inside...
"LITTLE BEAR! IT'S YOUR MOTHER!"
he exclaimed.

"MUMMY! My Mummy!" laughed Little Bear.
"We were really scared, Mummy! What's that in your bag?"

"Well, when I woke up this morning I was so hungry I decided to bake my favourite cake. Then I wondered if my Little Bear was hungry too, so I came to see you!"

"Oh, Mummy, you are so wonderful," said Little Bear, giving her a great big hug. "I was so hungry I ate up everything I had. Then I went to see all my friends and ate up everything they had."

"Never mind," said Mummy Bear. "I've brought lots of food in my big bag. There's enough for everyone until spring comes. Have some cake."

Little Bear grabbed two slices for himself.
Mummy Bear looked at him sternly.

" I forgot my manners," said Little Bear.
He offered it to all his friends.

They all enjoyed the cake. Then Badger started to yawn… and Squirrel yawned… and Hedgehog… and Beaver.

Squirrel asked, "Please may I sleep here?
I'm still a little bit worried about burglars."

Little Bear gave a great big yawn and they all headed off to bed.

Very soon they were all fast asleep. All, that is, except Fox.
He was outside, keeping watch.

Inside, Mummy Bear settled down to read a good book
in the armchair. But soon her eyes closed too.

Soon it was all quiet once more in the forest.